Grandpa Green

LANE SMITH

MACMILLAN CHILDREN'S BOOKS

First published in the USA 2011 by Roaring Brook Press
This edition published 2012 by Macmillan Children's Books
a division of Macmillan Publishers Limited
20 New Wharf Road, London N1 9RR
Basingstoke and Oxford
Associated companies throughout the world
www.panmacmillan.com

ISBN: 978-0-230-76645-7

Text and illustrations copyright © Lane Smith 2011
Book design by Molly Leach
Moral rights asserted.

A CIP catalogue record for this book is available from the British Library.

Printed in China

The inclusion of author website addresses in this book does not constitute an endorsement by or an association with Macmillan
Publishers of such sites or the content, products, advertising or other materials presented on such sites.

9 8 7 6 5 4 3 2 1

He was born a really long time ago,

before computers or mobile phones or television.

He grew up on a farm with
pigs and corn and carrots . . .

and eggs.

In nursery school
he got chicken pox.*

*Not from the chickens.

He had to stay home from school.
So he read stories about secret gardens
and wizards and a little engine that could.

In junior school

he stole his first kiss.

After senior school his wish was to study horticulture,

but he went to a world war instead.

He met his future
wife in a little café.

When the war was over, they were married.

They had many happy years
together and never, ever fought.

At least to hear *him* tell it.

They had children, lots more grandchildren,
and a great-grandchild, me.

He used to remember everything.

Now he's pretty old

and he sometimes forgets things

like his favourite floppy straw hat.

But the important stuff,

the garden remembers for him.